Welcome to
Little Funnies

Little Funnies is a delightful collection of picture books made to put a giggle into storytime.

There are funny stories about a laughing lobster, a daring mouse, a teeny tiny woman, and lots more colourful characters!

Perfect for sharing, these rib-tickling tales will have your little ones coming back for more!

TEE HEE!

HA HA !

For the cousins – Abby, Amelia,
Andrea, Ellen and Megan
P.R.

To my great-nephews – the twins,
Rupert and Charlie – with love
H.C.

First published 1998 by Walker Books Ltd
87 Vauxhall Walk, London SE11 5HJ

The edition published 2007

10 9 8 7 6 5 4 3 2 1

Text © 1998 Phyllis Root
Illustrations © 1998 Helen Craig

The moral rights of the author/illustrator
have been asserted.

This book has been typeset in Calligraphic Antique.

Printed in China

British Library Cataloguing in
Publication Data:
a catalogue record for this book is
available from the British Library

ISBN: 978-1-4063-0784-9

www.walkerbooks.co.uk

TURNOVER TUESDAY

Written by
Phyllis Root

Illustrated by
Helen Craig

WALKER BOOKS
AND SUBSIDIARIES

LONDON · BOSTON · SYDNEY · AUCKLAND

One Tuesday Bonnie Bumble baked **six** plum turnovers for breakfast.

"Delicious," she said,
and she ate up five,
every bite.

There wasn't even a crumb
left over for her little
dog, Spot.

But when Bonnie Bumble got up from her chair, she turned over upside down.

And nothing
could turn her
back over again.

So Bonnie Bumble put
her hat on her feet
and her shoes on
her hands.

Then she went
to do her chores.

Upside down she
milked the cow.

But the milk
SPLASHED out
of the bucket.

Upside down she gathered the eggs.

But the eggs SMASHED out of the basket.

On the way back to
the house, the sheep
nibbled her hair.

And the pig's tail
tickled her ear.

"This will never do!"
said Bonnie Bumble.

Back into the kitchen she
went to find the last
plum turnover.

Upside down she ate it,
almost every bite.

When she got up from
the table, she turned
back over,

right
side
up!

"Thank goodness everything's back to normal," said Bonnie Bumble.

And it was ...

except for Spot,
who had eaten
up all the crumbs.